ALASKA WILDLIFE
a coloring book
with illustrations and information
on 20 of Alaska's best known animals

Illustrated by Betsy Lee Holen
Written by Susan Dell Holen
Edited and produced by Anne Marie Holen

Copyright ©1988 by Betsy, Anne, and Susan Holen. Fourteenth printing 2006.

All rights reserved. No part of this publication may be reproduced in any form without prior written permission of the publisher. Published by Paisley Publishing, P.O. Box 142424, Anchorage, Alaska 99514. Alaska telephone and fax: 907/272-6604. Outside of Alaska: 423/870-8890.

ISBN 0-922127-00-X
Printed in the U.S.A.

Moose

Moose are big and heavy. They are the largest deer in the world, and the Alaskan moose is the largest moose. The largest male moose (called bulls) can weigh almost a ton, and have antlers as big as six feet from tip to tip. In the fall, the bull moose use their antlers to fight with each other. They fight over the female moose. Then they lose their antlers in the winter, growing new ones in the spring.

Most moose calves are born during the very end of May and the very beginning of June. People know that spring has come to Alaska when they all of a sudden start seeing a lot of mother moose with their new calves.

Moose calves grow extremely fast—up to 100 pounds a month for the first four months of life. They drink their mother's milk, and soon begin eating leaves, pond weeds, and other plants. Sometimes moose eat just about all day long.

Moose protect themselves from wolves, bears, and other predators by fighting with their hooves and antlers, and by running. Also, their huge size makes them difficult prey. Predators such as bears and wolves sometimes do get moose for food, though.

Moose don't seem to mind being near places where a lot of people live, if that is the best place to find food. In the winter especially, they can be seen in people's yards, eating twigs from the trees and bushes. In warmer weather, moose like to spend time in swampy areas called muskeg. They wade in and stick their heads underwater to find nutritious plants to eat. In the middle of a vast muskeg there might be a large relaxed group of moose, because wolves and bears usually don't go into the muskeg. It's easy for moose to travel in the watery muskeg because their legs are long and their feet are big.

Lynx

Lynx are the only cats native to Alaska. In other states there are other kinds of wild cats, but in Alaska there is only the lynx. They have extremely thick fur and big feet for running on the snow. They are larger than domestic cats—house cats weigh up to 15 pounds; lynx weigh up to 35 pounds.

Lynx kittens are born in June in a natural shelter the mother lynx has found, such as a cave or upturned tree root. They look a lot like house kittens, but they grow bigger faster. Baby lynx are blind at birth and totally helpless. The mother lynx stays with them at all times at this early age. Their eyes are developed enough to open after about two weeks. After this time, the mother will go out to hunt for food.

Just like other predators, the young lynx learn to hunt by playing and watching others hunt. Their survival depends on finding and catching prey. In their first winter of life, the kittens are almost full grown. They have learned how to hunt, and they have all their teeth. They are ready to go out on their own.

Lynx live mostly on snowshoe hares but also eat other small animals. Lynx like to travel alone and hunt at night. It is unusual to see a lynx during the day. Like other cats, they are quiet, patient, and powerful hunters. If there aren't many hares to eat, mother lynx aren't very healthy and therefore don't have many babies. The lynx population decreases, and eventually the number of hares in the forest increases again. When there is an abundance of hares, the lynx population also increases. And so this cycle continues.

Caribou

Caribou are most often seen crossing the open tundra. As many as 10,000 caribou will travel together. They travel constantly. They are strong swimmers, and big rivers don't stop them. They are also good climbers, so they travel across the foothills of mountains.

Caribou, like moose, are members of the deer family. They are a soft brown color, with white fur on their necks, rumps, and feet. Female and male caribou grow antlers. This is very unusual—in other deer species, only the male has antlers. The male caribou's antlers grow up to four feet from base to tip. In the late fall, the male caribou lose their antlers, and the females lose theirs in late spring. Then they grow a new pair. In some parts of Alaska, it is common to see many bleached bone-white caribou antlers scattered about the tundra.

In the spring, caribou travel to the calving grounds, a place where the wind has blown away the snow and there is plenty of food. There the cows have their young. Caribou calves weigh only about 12 pounds when they are born, but they grow quickly and can run almost immediately. Running is important because they depend on their speed to survive—they run to escape from wolves and other predators. Being in such a large group is also important for protection. And both females and males can use their antlers to defend themselves and their young against attack.

Caribou prefer to eat lichen, which grows on the open tundra, and other vegetation. In the far north, where most caribou live, plants are small and tough because of the extremely cold winters. This is the kind of vegetation caribou like to eat.

Caribou herds stay together throughout generations. Some herds live near the sea, some live near the mountains. During the summer they look for windy areas or cold places to get away from bugs.

Wolves

Wolves travel in packs all over Alaska and on many of its islands. Packs usually have fewer than ten wolves, but can have as many as 30. Throughout the days, they travel over their territory. If the animals they hunt are abundant, the pack's territory is small, and the wolves spend a lot of time relaxing and playing. But if food is scarce, wolf packs may travel hundreds of miles, searching and hunting. Sometimes the pack will break up and wolves will travel alone or in small groups for a while. At night they howl across the distances to each other.

Wolves eat moose, caribou, deer, smaller animals like mice, and sometimes even birds. When they hunt larger animals, wolves usually kill the ones that are already weak or injured, although by hunting in packs they are sometimes able to bring down healthy ones as well. They help keep the moose and caribou populations from becoming too large, which can lead to starvation when there is not enough food to go around.

Wolves have their young in dens in the spring. The mother wolf usually has about five pups, although a healthy female wolf may have as many as ten pups if hunting has been good that year and she has had plenty to eat. Wolf pups are playful, like dog pups. Since their survival depends on hunting, wolf pups play hunting games.

Wolves give their pups food, love, hunting lessons, and protection. Wolves within a pack are dependent upon each other. Some are leaders, some watch the pups, some are good runners, and some bring food back from the hunt to the ones that stay behind. The wolf that brings back food for the pups has already eaten it. She brings it up from her stomach. That way it has become soft enough for the pups to eat.

Sometimes when wolf pups are playing, they will grab on to their mother's tail with their teeth, and drag behind her as she tries to walk. After a while the mother gets tired of it and snarls at them so they will stop. Then they go play with something else.

Dall Sheep

Dall sheep live on the highest cliffs and ridges above the tree line, often even above the clouds. Few people get close enough to see them; they only see white dots on a mountain side.

As soon as grass appears on the lower mountain sides in the spring, Dall sheep come down to feed on it. Life is easier in the spring, summer, and fall. In the winter, deep snow may force Dall sheep to live on just a few mountain ridges often blasted by extremely high winds. Many die over the winter from falling, being caught in avalanches, and starvation. But in the spring when the snow melts, their range becomes large and food once again becomes plentiful. They travel about grazing in the warmer weather.

As spring progresses into summer, the herd of sheep again moves higher into the rugged mountains. Along the way, the female sheep (ewes) stop to have their babies. The males (rams) keep going farther up into the high country. The ewes and rams don't come together again until the fall.

The group of pregnant ewes look for hard-to-reach places with soft grassy spots to have their young. The steeper it is, the less chance that wolves and other predators will hunt there. The mother Dall sheep usually has one white lamb, which only weighs about seven pounds—the size of a small house cat. Right away it tries to walk and soon it is climbing, sometimes using its mother to climb on for practice. It is important to learn to climb because climbing in the steepest places is the Dall sheep's best defense against predators.

In the fall, when Dall sheep sense the winter coming on, the ewes and lambs join the rams. Now they are all together. Over the summer they have had plenty of bunch grass, sedges, willows, and lichen to eat. By this time, Dall sheep, like other land animals, have grown thick fur to help keep them warm in the winter. The lambs have gone from seven to about 60 pounds. Most important, they have learned how to climb.

Ptarmigan

Ptarmigan live all over Alaska, from the tundra to the edge of the sea and even high in the mountains. In Alaska, there are three different kinds of ptarmigan: willow ptarmigan, rock ptarmigan, and white-tailed ptarmigan. The willow ptarmigan is the Alaska state bird.

Willow ptarmigan build their nests on the ground, and spend much of their lives on the ground. The female looks for a nesting place under a log, inside a clump of grass, or under bushes. She digs a hole and lines the nest with soft things she finds. Then she lays one egg a day for about seven days. The eggs are usually light tan with reddish spots. When the mother ptarmigan goes away from the nest, she covers the eggs with grass and leaves. The rest of the time she sits on them to keep them warm. In about 21 days the chicks have grown enough to peck their way out of the eggs.

Lynx, foxes, eagles, owls, and ravens are some of the predators which eat ptarmigan and their eggs. If an animal approaches the nest, the mother will sit very still, making it hard to see her. If the animal comes nearer, she will suddenly fall over and flop around on the ground, as if wounded. This way the predator will go after her instead of the eggs. At the last moment she will fly into the air.

Ptarmigan are protected both summer and winter by the color of their feathers. In the summer they have brown feathers which blend with the branches of bushes, logs, and dead grass. In the fall they lose many of their feathers and grow snow-white ones. They also grow feathers on their feet for warmth and long toenails for running around on hard snowdrifts. They can hide themselves in an instant. One way they hide is to fly into a group of bushes and sink down into the soft snow.

Huge groups of ptarmigan gather before their migration in the fall. If you were to walk up to a group, they would all fly straight up into the air at the same time. Ptarmigan do not migrate as far as some other birds—maybe only a few miles, down to lower elevations where the winter weather is less severe.

Wolverines

Although wolverines live all over Alaska, they are seldom seen. They roam over large areas and are never very plentiful. Wolverines watch, smell, and listen for danger constantly. If a person sees a wolverine, it is usually gone so fast the person is likely to think it vanished into thin air.

Wolverines eat just about anything they can get their teeth into—plants like blueberries, and any animal they hunt or find dead. If wolves, coyotes, or black bears kill an animal, a wolverine will find it using its sense of smell. Even though the wolverine is smaller, it will try to scare off the other animals. Wolverines often succeed because they are tough, strong, fierce, and don't give up, and the other animals know this.

They do hunt, but their legs are too short for them to run fast enough to catch healthy grown animals very easily. Sometimes they surprise young or sick animals. After they eat, they carry the leftovers away to hide them. All the other meat-eating animals in the area can smell these food caches and will rob them— as long as the wolverine is not there!

Wolverines have also been known to break into people's caches and cabins. They are strong and persistent and will spend a long time finding a way in. Once inside, they tear into everything, looking for food.

In late winter the female has her kits. Usually two to four kits are born, tiny and helpless. By the following spring, the kits have grown and learned much about life. They go with their mother everywhere, playing most of the time they are awake. By the time wolverine babies are adults (after about one year), they have developed very strong teeth and jaws and strong neck muscles used for pulling things apart.

Wolverines travel over large distances, crossing glaciers and rivers, climbing high into mountains and going out upon the open tundra. They live in dens which they have made in hollow tree stumps, abandoned beaver lodges, and rock piles. Wolverines are active all year long—they don't hibernate.

Trumpeter Swans

The graceful trumpeter swan is the largest swan in the world. Some trumpeters live on the tundra, others live on land that has been flattened by glaciers. On the tundra and glacial flatlands are many shallow lakes and ponds, and each swan family has one. Their large nest is made out of feathers, moss, grass, and lichen. Sometimes they find an empty beaver lodge in their pond and build their nest on top of it. Sometimes they build their nest so it floats on the water.

The female swan lays about five eggs in the spring. For 31 days she keeps them under her, warming them so the babies inside can develop. Whenever she leaves the nest, she covers the eggs with grass. She must leave the nest for a while to graze on grass and other plants. Sometimes swans eat at night. A bright moon might shine on a pair of swans as they graze along the edges of their pond.

When baby trumpeter swans peck their way out of eggs, they are light gray and weigh about 7 ounces. They spend the next few months paddling in the water, following their mother around, and learning what plants are good to eat. They can't fly yet, but they flap their wings a lot. By fall they are much bigger and long flight feathers have grown on their wings. They begin trying to fly. At first it is hard to get off the surface of the pond. They keep trying. They have to be able to fly by fall, so they can migrate south before the pond freezes over.

Trumpeter swans gather together in groups before migrating. They fly in a long line or in a V-shape, on their way to southeastern Alaska and the coast of British Columbia, up to 1000 miles. In the fall you might see them, and hear a sound you will never forget—the loud trumpet sound of the graceful trumpeter swan, going out over the marshes on a cool fall day.

Musk Ox

Long ago, musk ox lived all over Alaska. But then the musk ox were being hunted too heavily. They were all killed off. By 1850, the last herd had disappeared.

The musk ox would have remained extinct in Alaska if someone hadn't decided in 1935 to get some from another northern country—Greenland—and bring them to Alaska.

The people who brought them back let them go on Nunivak Island because they thought there would be plenty for them to eat there and that the weather would be about right for musk ox. Those people were right. Musk ox still live on cold, misty Nunivak Island and now in other places around Alaska.

Musk ox are somewhat similar to cattle and other grazing animals. They just like to eat, breed, raise their young, and sleep. Domestic animals which people raise in pens and pastures don't usually have to watch out for predators. But wild grazing animals do.

Musk ox stay together in small herds. Both bulls and cows care for the young and defend them against predators. If a wolf approaches, they will get all the calves together, make a circle around them, and face outward ready to fight. With lowered head the musk ox butts the wolf with its curved horns. The wolf goes flying, often suffering broken ribs. Or the musk ox will use its hooves. The circle defense is hard to penetrate and wolves and other predators will often just give up after a while.

Like most other wild animals in Alaska, musk ox breed in the fall so that the pregnant mother carries the baby inside her all winter. In the spring the calves are born.

The springtime is also the time when musk ox shed their under-fur which helped keep them warm in the freezing Alaska winter. This fur is so soft and warm that it is gathered by people who make it into sweaters and other beautiful garments. It is called "qiviut."

Snowy Owls

Home for snowy owls is on frozen marshes, prairies, and open tundra. Little brown rodents called lemmings live there and lemmings are what snowy owls like to eat.

Snowy owls build their nests on the tops of bumps on the tundra. Building the nest doesn't take much work. The female snowy owl gathers a few feathers and a few bits of moss, just enough to keep the eggs from rolling off the bump onto the wet, soggy tundra.

The female lays about six white eggs. While she keeps them warm, the male hunts. He brings food back to the nest for her. After the owlets are born, the male brings small mice and birds and the mother feeds them to the babies.

The baby owls hatch at different times, so the nest is filled with babies of different sizes. At first, each owlet is covered with soft white feathers called "down." Before winter, new feathers begin to push the downy feathers out. During all this time the owlets rarely leave the nest. They can't fly and they can't even walk around very well. No animal can get near the babies without risking getting hurt by the mother owl's curved beak and sharp talons.

The owlets must learn how to hunt by the first winter in order to survive. By winter they have their flight feathers and strong wing muscles. And they have keen eyes that can see things from far away.

In the early evening, snowy owls perch on a little hill, silent and still, hardly blinking an eye. They watch for little animals in the field. When they see one, they push off the ground and immediately they are flying effortlessly and silently. In the winter they glide just above the surface of the snow.

When the owl catches the animal it eats it whole. Later, after the owl's stomach has digested all the meat, the owl coughs up a ball made of the animal's fur and bones. Scientists (and school children) have reconstructed whole animal skeletons from these balls.

Polar Bears

Polar bears live in the Arctic, the far north where it is extremely cold, and the colors are whites, blues, and pale shades of sunrise. They like ice and they live on huge "islands" of ice that drift slowly in the northern ocean. They blend right in with the white landscape all around them.

Polar bears like to live, hunt, and travel alone. They hunt for seals and seals are about all they ever eat. The blubbery seal meat helps them grow fat. Along with their extremely thick fur, the fat helps them tolerate temperatures down to and beyond 60 degrees below zero.

Just before winter sets in, the pregnant polar bear begins to look for a place to den. She leaves the ice and travels onto the snow-covered tundra. There, she scrapes out a deep dip in the snow, and as snow continues to fall, it covers her. The warmth of her body melts the snow around her and soon she has formed a warm ice cave. Usually only pregnant females stay in dens. Other polar bears may have dens in the winter, but they don't spend as much time in them.

The cubs are born in December. Most often, the mother bear has two cubs. The tiny cubs weigh about one pound. The mother and cubs stay in the den the rest of the winter. By springtime the cubs are pudgy from drinking their mother's milk, and the mother is hungry.

After the mother and cubs break out of their snow cave, they stay near the den for several days. The mother wants the babies to get used to being out in the open world. Then they travel to the ocean and the ice. The mother begins to hunt for seals. The cubs stay with her for two years, playing, sleeping, learning how to hunt, and getting strong.

Summer or winter, polar bears are where there is sea ice. In the spring they travel farther north to be on stable sea ice. This means in the summer they are on the most northern part of the earth, where it is cold all the time.

Walrus

Upon the Arctic ocean lie huge slowly drifting islands of ice, called pack ice. This pack ice is where walrus like to be. Walrus, some weighing as much as six horses (4,000 pounds), are kept warm by all their blubber. Walrus are clumsy out of the water, but in the water they are sleek and fast. Walrus use their tusks to climb over ice ridges, for fights, and for emergencies. Such an emergency would be if a baby walrus was caught in a deep ice crack; the mother walrus would use her tusks to break the ice apart.

Walruses have whiskers covering the front of their faces. Walruses feel the ocean bottom with their face and whiskers, finding food such as clams, snails, crabs, shrimp, and worms in the mud.

In the winter, walrus live in the southern Arctic near Bristol Bay. They begin to travel north in the spring, swimming and resting, following the edge of the pack ice as it melts in the warming weather. Along the way, the males stop and the pregnant females continue on to the place where they have their calves.

A baby walrus is born on the ice. It must stay next to the mother, using warmth from her body to keep from freezing. A newborn walrus weighs about 100 pounds and is dark gray. By age 2 it weighs as much as 800 pounds (the same as a small horse) and has turned reddish brown. During those two years, the calf and mother stay close. The mother protects the calf. If the calf is sick, the mother walrus will not leave it. Even if it dies, the mother walrus will stay with it for many days before giving up on it.

By the end of summer, the walrus have reached the northern coast of Alaska. They rest for a while, and then begin traveling again, back the way they came, as the pack ice freezes farther and farther south in the cooling weather.

Belugas

Belugas are small white whales, weighing only about one ton. They are found in the far northern waters of the Bering Sea and the Chukchi and Arctic Oceans, and farther south in Cook Inlet and Yakutat Bay. Unlike another white mammal of the far north, the polar bear, belugas are always found in groups. They seem to enjoy each other's company. In the fall as they are migrating, hundreds of them will gather in an annual reunion.

Belugas are also known as "sea canaries" because of all the "singing" they do. They make many different squealing, chirping, whistling, and clicking sounds. These sounds are so loud that people can hear them through the bottom of boats! Just about the only other sounds heard in this frozen region of the globe are the groaning and crackling of sea ice and the wind blowing over it.

Belugas live in the coldest ocean of the world, the Arctic, which covers the northern portion of the earth. Ice covers most of the Arctic. Yet belugas are warm-blooded, like humans (not like fish, whose blood stays the same temperature as the water around them). How do belugas keep warm enough? Like other sea mammals which live in cold water, they have a very thick layer of blubber which insulates them.

Babies are born light brown with light gray spots. As they mature, they become creamy white. Belugas are the only white whales in the world. They are also the only whales able to turn their heads from side to side. Belugas and all whales are protective of each other, especially the young. If one whale gets hurt and can't swim, the other whales will swim alongside of it, trying to keep it on the surface where it can breathe.

Belugas like to live in shallow water near the shore or in inlets and river outlets. In the fall, when they migrate south, they can even be seen hundreds of miles up great rivers like the Yukon. In the shallow ocean waters and rivers, they find what they like to eat—fish and smaller organisms. There is also more light in shallow water, so the belugas can see what they are hunting. Although it is not uncommon to see belugas migrating, no one knows for sure where these mammals spend their winters.

Silver Salmon

Salmon start as orange eggs buried in the gravel of a swift stream. They hatch into tiny clear fishes. As the days go by, the stream carries them toward the ocean.

Baby salmon eat insect eggs. When they reach the end of the stream where it flows into the sea, they have gotten stronger. At this time they are barely larger than a person's finger. This is when the young salmon begin their travels.

Silver salmon spend two to three years as travelers in the sea, eating smaller creatures and growing bigger. They swim toward the Arctic Ocean in the spring, and toward the ocean near California in the fall. They swim deep when there is a storm. When there are lots of floating bugs and other things to eat, they swim just under the surface. Sometimes they jump above the surface.

Many animals like to eat salmon. Muskrats, owls, and sandpipers eat baby salmon in the streams. Fishermen in boats take them out of the sea in big nets. Seals, sea lions, porpoise, and killer whales catch them and eat them. After three years, when they return to their streams to spawn, eagles, bears, humans, and other animals are waiting for them on the shore.

By the time they reach their streams, the salmon are strong and silvery. They are strong enough to swim against the flowing stream. As they travel up the stream they begin to lose their silvery color. Their sides turn red. Then the salmon stop eating. Finally they get to the place where they were born. The female digs a hole in the gravel with her tail, and lays the orange eggs in the hole. The male is ready and deposits a white covering over the eggs, which fertilizes them so they can grow. The male and female use their last energy to drive away intruders. Then they die.

Looking down on Alaska from the sky, you can see hundreds of rivers and streams winding their way around mountains and through the open grasslands and tundra, going to the sea. Many of the streams have salmon eggs, baby salmon, or spawning salmon in them, depending on the time of year.

Bald Eagles

Bald eagles use up to 2,000 pounds of sticks, carried one-by-one, to build their nests. Each spring the same pair of eagles, a male and a female, returns to the nest. Building a new nest each spring would be too much work. They fix it up with a new lining of spruce boughs or seaweed and other soft materials. The nest has to be large enough to hold them, their eggs or young ones, and any food brought back.

Bald eagles usually lay two eggs shortly after they arrive in the spring and have fixed up the nest. The eggs hatch in early summer, when days are warmer and the scenery is getting green. Baby eagles are scrawny and totally helpless. The mother eagle is extremely protective of the eaglets. With her powerful beak and sharp talons, she will viciously attack anything that comes too near the nest.

Two months after hatching, the eaglets have grown strong wing muscles and long wing feathers and are ready to try flying. During this time, the mother eagle sits on a nearby branch anxiously watching.

Until the eaglet is a skilled hunter, it must eat scraps left after the adult eagles have eaten. It takes about two years of learning for a young eagle to become a skilled hunter. During salmon-spawning time, eaglets can wade into the river and grab the weakest salmon that are about to die.

Eagles hunt animals like marmots and hares, and birds such as ducks by swooping down from the sky and grabbing them with their claws, called talons. Eagles are also scavengers, eating animals which have died from disease or accidents.

In the late summer and fall, the eagle's main diet is salmon. Eagles and bears are seen at this time catching and devouring spawning and dying fish. Up to six fish a day are eaten by each eagle. Between meals they rest in the nearby trees. Seagulls and other animals sneak in and grab a piece when they can.

Eagles have a keen sense of sight—they can see a mouse in a meadow from a mile away. Flying higher than most birds can go, they look for things below. They can travel extremely fast flying in the wind.

Brown Bears

Brown bears and grizzly bears are nearly the same. Brown bears live near the ocean and grizzlies live inland. In the fall, bears are so fat that they appear to waddle. This is because they eat all summer in order to gain enough weight to last all winter while they sleep or hibernate. Bears rarely eat in the winter. In the spring they look skinny.

Bears start looking for their dens in the fall, when leaves have fallen from the trees and nights are bitter cold. They dig their own dens or look for natural shelters on hillsides or mountain slopes. They line the den with soft grasses and leaves. Then one day, they crawl inside. They spend the winter in their dens. If it is a warm winter day, a bear might come out of the den to look around and maybe spend a little time foraging for food.

The cubs are born in the middle of winter in the den. They are no bigger than a mouse, and they have no fur. Usually a mother bear has two cubs, but may have as many as four. They grow quickly and by spring they are ready to come out of the den.

When they first come out of their dens in the spring, bears look for areas to live where there are meadows or large open grasslands. They eat a lot of grass this time of year. They also eat berries and other plants. Bears are omnivorous—they eat both plants and meat. Most of the meat brown bears eat is salmon. They also eat the remains of animals that they find that have died. Sometimes they spend a lot of time catching rodents, such as marmots, to eat. Bears will also kill and eat moose or caribou, especially calves. They even eat insect eggs and grubs they find in the ground. They have to eat a lot all summer long.

By mid-summer, brown bears come together at rivers where salmon are spawning. They swim, wade, or just stand by the bank waiting for fish to come by. They are good at catching fish by jumping on them or swatting them out of the river with their big paws. Mother bears fish for their young cubs. When the cubs get older, they feed on scraps left behind by other bears until they get better at fishing themselves. Then they may fight with adult bears for the good fishing spots.

Puffins

Puffins are very colorful birds that live on the sea and on the cliffs that rise from the sea. Compared to most birds, puffins are not good at flying. They are so heavy that when they take off from a cliff, they fall a long ways before they get enough speed to fly. They flap their wings as fast as they can. Sometimes when they land on the water, they almost look like they are out of control. They always land hard, so they only land on water or on soft grass.

But puffins are made for flying under water. In the water, they use their wings as paddles and they steer with their legs. Puffins dive into the deep water and stay down for several minutes. They catch the tiny silver fish. Then they pop up to the surface. Sometimes they struggle into the air, kicking and paddling the water to gain speed for take-off, and carry the mouthful of food back to their young ones.

In the winter, puffins move out on the ocean, far away from land. Here they float on the water in groups all winter. They continue to fly to where the fish are, and swim under water to catch them. They have lost their colorful beaks and legs. Instead, their beaks have turned from bright orange and yellow to grayish orange and their legs are dull instead of bright orange. In late winter, puffins lose some of their feathers and grow new ones. Some of the feathers they lose are the flight feathers. These are the long feathers all birds have in their wings. Until their new flight feathers grow in, puffins can't fly at all. They have to be in a safe place at this time. They won't be able to fly for a few weeks.

In the spring, when sunlight is sparkling on the water, puffins return to their colonies on the sea cliffs. For a day or so they rest after the long flight. They have grown bright beak parts again and have their colorful legs back. This makes them attractive to each other. Each one pairs up with its mate, and they find their old burrow which is a hole they have dug in the dirt and lined with feathers and grass. In the cozy burrow, the female puffin lays two or three eggs. Both the male and female sit on the eggs to keep them warm until they hatch, and when the baby puffins are born, both parents take care of them.

Spotted Seals

Spotted seals live in the sea and on the ice. Their bodies are made for swimming fast to get away from killer whales and for chasing fish. They fold their front flippers along their sides and stretch out their back flippers. Their bodies bend back and forth like a fish to push through the water. Spotted seals don't even have ears on the outside of their heads to slow them down, just two tiny holes.

In the early spring, the pregnant females look for blocks of ice that are floating by the edge of the pack ice. The mother jumps out of the water onto one. This is where the spotted seal pup is born. You might see several seal pups with their mothers gently floating on the water on their blocks of ice. They feel safe there. The polar bears don't like to swim out to them and the killer whales don't like to swim among the heavy, sharp pieces of ice.

The spotted seal pup is born with a woolly white coat, but it doesn't have enough blubber to keep it warm. It goes from inside the warm mother to air that can be colder than 20 degrees below zero. The mother stays by it to keep it warm. By drinking its mother's milk, it begins to grow and get a thick layer of blubber. Soon it is swimming in the sea and playing with its mother. It nips at her flippers, chases her, and sometimes rides on her back. This way it learns how to swim and dodge and dive. It can get away from predators. It also swims between boulders where killer whales can't fit. When a killer whale comes near, the mother slaps the water with her flipper to warn the pup.

By August, the baby has its adult coat. It is pale silver with dots of dark gray and silvery black. After about a year, the seal pup begins to spend more and more time away from its mother, playing with other seals and sleeping other places. The mother is pregnant with a new baby. At one year old, the pup has learned how to take care of itself. It has become a skilled swimmer and can catch the salmon and other fish that travel past.

Killer Whales

Killer whales, sometimes called orcas (from their scientific name *Orcinus orca*) are known for their beautiful black and white coloring. They are called killer whales because they are the only whale known to eat warm-blooded animals, such as seals, sea lions, and porpoises, in addition to fish.

However, killer whales are not people eaters. In fact, they are curious about people and sometimes like to swim over to boats. The whales seem to be wondering about the people as much as the people are wondering about them. People can put on diving suits and swim among the killer whales. This is how people found out that orcas are friendly, intelligent animals.

In the wild, killer whales like to be in small groups (called "pods"). They communicate underwater with sounds like "tick . . . click . . . eeeeeee . . ." Whale voices are interesting to listen to, and some people have studied them for many years to try to learn what the whales are saying to each other.

Most animals on land use their sense of vision to see what is around them. There is plenty of light on land. In the sea there is not so much light. The deeper you go, the less light there is, and the harder it is to see. Whales use their sense of hearing more than their sense of vision. They make a sound and they can tell by the way it echoes back to them exactly what is around them and where they are.

Whales breathe air, like we do. The whale has a hole in the top of its head which it breathes through every time it comes to the surface—about every 30 seconds. A grown killer whale can weigh as much as eight tons (about as much as 100 adult male humans), so you can imagine how big a breath of air it takes. Its lungs are huge.

Killer whale calves weigh as much as 400 pounds at birth and can be almost seven feet long. Just as soon as the baby is born, it goes up to the surface to get a breath of air. It already knows how to swim. Orca babies, like all mammals, drink their mother's milk for nourishment to grow. Later they learn to hunt and become meat eaters.

Sea Otters

Sea otters are at home in the sea. They float on their backs on the water even if the sea is stormy. They play in the waves. They hardly ever get out of the sea. On the bottom of the sea they find sea urchins, crabs, and octopus. They pick them up in their paws and swim to the surface. At the surface the otter takes a big breath. Then it floats on its back, sets the food on its chest, and eats. It takes several deep breaths and dives again.

Other animals that live in cold water have a layer of blubber which keeps them warm. But sea otters don't have blubber, even though each sea otter eats about 25 pounds of food a day. Sea otters have a thick coat of fur to keep them warm. Their fur is so thick that water doesn't touch their skin. If they get crab juice or octopus ink in their fur, they clean it out. Clean fur won't clump up and let water in.

The mother sea otter keeps her baby's fur clean. Most of the time the pup lays on its mother's chest. It sleeps there, drinks the mother's milk there, and even plays there. When the mother dives for food, she leaves the baby floating on its back. The baby can't swim or dive. It can only float. If the pup drifts away or the mother comes to the surface in a different place, the pup cries a high sound. The mother and pup call to each other until the mother finds the pup.

After the pup is born until it is ready to be on its own, it watches its mother to learn how to swim, dive, and keep itself clean. Otters learn that if they have a crab with a thick shell, they can get a rock to smash the shell. Then they scoop out the tasty insides.

Otters like to play. They are excellent swimmers and will chase each other through the water. Sometimes they can be seen rolling over and over in the water, or playing with the round balloon-like ends of kelp. They play until they get tired or feel it's time to eat.

Glossary

avalanche
a fall or slide of a large mass of snow or rock down a mountainside

blubber
the thick layer of fat between the skin and muscle layers of whales, seals, and other sea mammals

cache
a hiding place for food or supplies

carnivorous
flesh-eating or predatory

domestic
living with human beings; tame

extinct
no longer existing in living form

flight feathers
the longest, broadest, strongest feathers all flying birds have in their wings

forage
to wander around searching for food

glacier
an extended mass of ice formed from snow moving very slowly down from high mountains. The ice on the bottom of a glacier is formed from snow which fell thousands of years ago.

graze
to feed on growing grasses or other vegetation

grubs
the thick, wormlike larva of certain insects

herbivorous
feeding entirely on plants or plant parts

hibernate
to pass the winter in a dormant (sleep-like) state

insulate
to protect against loss of heat

kelp
a very large, brownish seaweed that attaches on one end to the ocean floor and has an air-filled bulb which floats on the other end

mammals
animals, including humans, which have bodies that regulate heat to keep warm and in which the female produces milk

migrate
> to move from one region to another, especially in a large group on a regular basis

muskeg
> large areas of shallow, mossy swamps in northern areas

native
> being born and living in a certain place; an original inhabitant

omnivorous
> eating both animal and plant substances

pack ice
> ice on the sea which is several feet thick and covers many miles of the ocean's surface

predator
> an animal that lives by hunting and killing other animals for food

prey
> any creature hunted or caught for food

qiviut
> the soft underfur of the musk ox used for making into yarn and knitting into clothing

rodent
> an animal such as a mouse, rat, squirrel, or beaver, characterized by large front teeth adapted for knawing or nibbling

scavenger
> an animal that feeds on dead or decaying matter

sedges
> plants resembling grasses but having solid rather than hollow stems

spawn
> to produce many offspring (usually used to describe fish laying eggs)

talon
> the claw of a predatory bird

thicket
> a dense growth of shrubs or underbrush

tundra
> a treeless area in arctic regions, with a permanently frozen subsoil and supporting low-growing vegetation

About this book:

Three sisters created this book: one writing, one illustrating and one publishing, when desk-top publishing was brand-new. Betsy, the artist, has a bachelor of fine arts degree from the University of Alaska and is now a free-lance fine artist. She has been drawing animals since the age of three. Susan, the writer, has a bachelor's degree in elementary education from the University of New Mexico. This was her first book. She has since written two more natural history books for children (see below), and is working on a book about her years at an Alaskan lodge. Anne Marie typeset this book on a computer located in the loft of a tiny cabin high on a bluff above Homer, Alaska. The first print run of 1500 copies was done at Fritz Creek Printing in Homer.

The cover illustrations were colored with high quality colored pencils. Crayons, felt-tip markers, and watercolor paints could also be used. Be careful with dark markers as they tend to be even darker when absorbed by the paper. Also, try not to put two dark colors right next to each other for things that you need to be able to tell apart. Don't use too much water with your water-colors; your brush should slide easily, but without letting go of too much water. You can use different colors than things really are, which can be fun, or you can use the coloring guide for accurate colors.

We would like to thank our parents for the "art table," the paints, the paper, the books, the hikes and camping trips, and everything else they provided us when we were kids to encourage our creativity and spirit of adventure. We also wish to thank Jacques Cousteau.

NATURAL HISTORY COLORING BOOKS AVAILABLE FROM PAISLEY PUBLISHING:

ALASKA WILDLIFE
Featuring 20 different Alaska animals from the land and sea in their natural habitat with a page of educational text with each drawing, for ages 8 and up.

ARCTIC ANIMAL BABIES
Featuring 36 baby animals of the world's Arctic region with a line or two of information about each animal and big, color-in titles, for children ages 3 and up.

THE ALASKA WOLF
A graduate student's day-to-day journal of wolf-watching, with 19 sketches to color, facts, and drawing lessons all about the Alaska wolf, for ages 10 and up.

To order, write the name of the books you would like, your name, and your address on a piece of paper. Send $7.95 each for *Alaska Wildlife* and *Arctic Animal Babies* and $9.95 each for *The Alaska Wolf* to: Paisley Publishing, P.O. Box 142424, Anchorage, Alaska 99514. Please send check or money order only. Prices include shipping and handling.